P9-DWP-998

Maughan's

The Would-be-Witch of Williamstown.

by story-teller Pat Traynor
illustrated by Carol Pelham-Thorman

Melbourne
OXFORD UNIVERSITY PRESS
Oxford   Wellington   New York

Oxford University Press

OXFORD LONDON GLASGOW
NEW YORK TORONTO MELBOURNE WELLINGTON
NAIROBI DAR ES SALAAM CAPE TOWN
KUALA LUMPUR SINGAPORE HONG KONG TOKYO
DELHI BOMBAY CALCUTTA MADRAS KARACHI

*This book is copyright. Apart from any fair
dealing for the purposes of private study,
research, criticism or review, as permitted under
the Copyright Act, no part may be reproduced
by any process without written permission.
Inquiries should be made to the publishers.*

© *Text Pat Traynor 1980*
© *Illustrations Carol Pelham-Thorman 1980*

First published 1980

National Library of Australia Cataloguing in
Publication Data

Traynor, Pat.
   The would-be-witch of Williamstown.

   For children
   ISBN 0 19 554243 6

   I. Pelham-Thorman, Carol, illus.
   II. Title.

A823'.3

Typography by Robin Cowpe
Typeset by Davey Litho Graphics Pty. Ltd.
Printed in Hong Kong
Published by Oxford University Press,
7 Bowen Crescent, Melbourne

This is a story about Mrs Pollywobble of Williamstown, who lives in a tiny bluestone cottage in . . . no, I'd better not tell you the name of the street.

The children of Williamstown thought Mrs Pollywobble was a *Witch,* but that was mainly because of her cat, Gingerbread, who seemed like a witch's cat. He had grey-green eyes, which flashed like forgotten dreams. Mrs Pollywobble took him for walks on a golden chain, and all the dogs in the town were afraid of him.

Now the children were almost right— Mrs Pollywobble was a *Would-be-Witch*, because she didn't quite know how to be a *real* one. (And if Gingerbread knew, he kept it to himself.) But she *did* have an old book of spells which she'd found in a rusty tin trunk on her back porch.

Some nights, when she was sitting by herself, Mrs Pollywobble would study the old book of spells. There was one spell she was very tempted to try, and she read it over and over again. It was called:

'How to make a MONSTER (friendly kind)'.

HOW TO MAKE A MONSTER
(friendly kind)

1 teaspoon of ground fingernails
4 leaves of fresh mint

2 tufts of hair from a black goat

1 tin of tomato soup

mix all these together over a hot stove and stir
vigorously with a pirate's wooden leg. chant
the MAGIC WORDS
Fingernails, soup and all that
Send me a creature who'll sit down and chat
Black is not black,
White is not white,
The place it comes from
Is far beyond night.

'How good it would be to have a friendly creature who could talk to me,' thought the Would-be-Witch. 'I've got all the things I need for the mixture, but where could I find a pirate's wooden leg?'

She wondered and wondered. Then one day she remembered an old man in Williamstown who had an attic full of junk. Perhaps he would have a pirate's wooden leg.

So she went to see him. Fortunately, he had a spare one, and he said she could borrow it for a week.

Now there was nothing to stop her.

The next night, Mrs Pollywobble collected all the things she needed and set them up on her back porch. She took out her oldest, most battered pot, plugged in her little electric stove, and began.

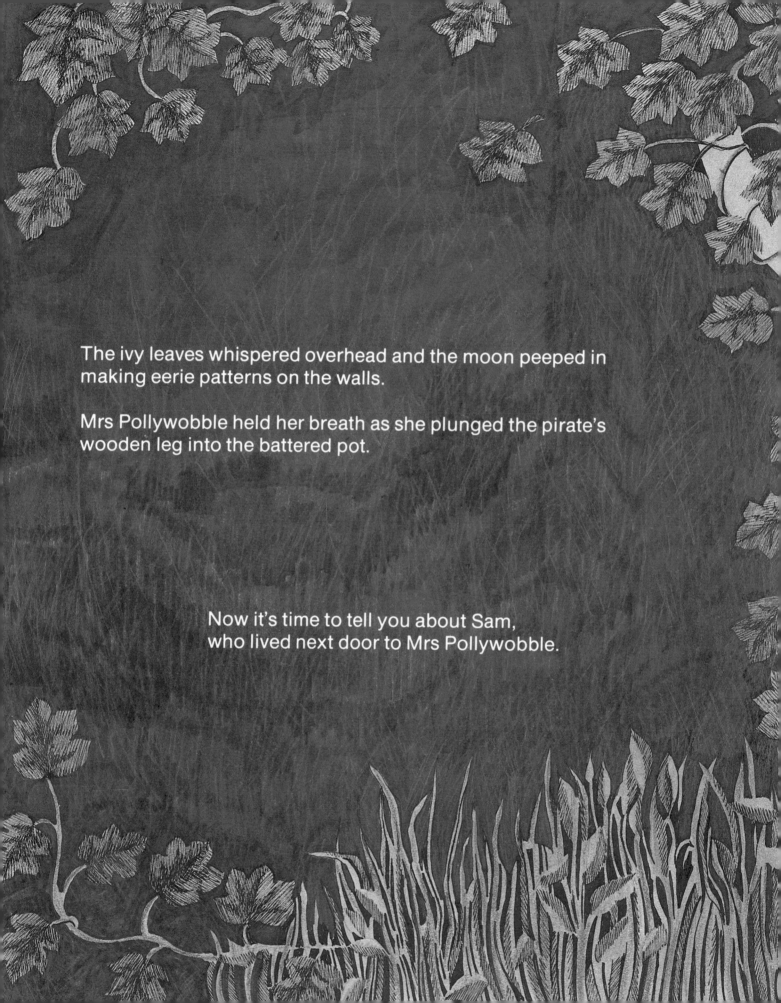

The ivy leaves whispered overhead and the moon peeped in making eerie patterns on the walls.

Mrs Pollywobble held her breath as she plunged the pirate's wooden leg into the battered pot.

Now it's time to tell you about Sam,
who lived next door to Mrs Pollywobble.

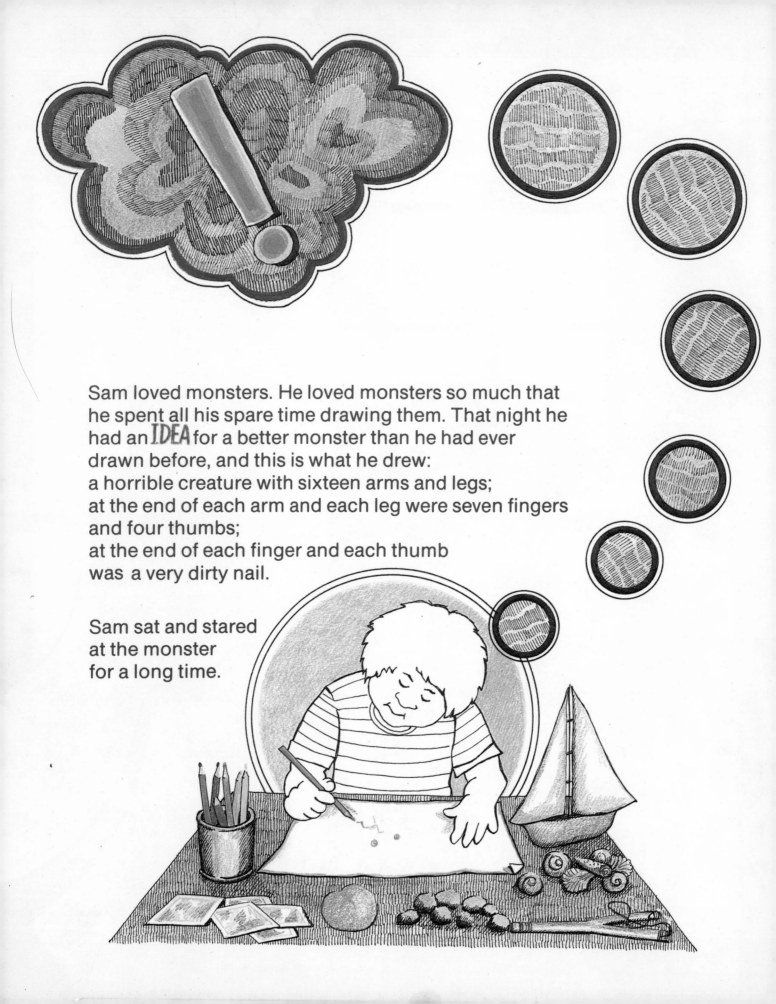

Sam loved monsters. He loved monsters so much that he spent all his spare time drawing them. That night he had an IDEA for a better monster than he had ever drawn before, and this is what he drew:
a horrible creature with sixteen arms and legs;
at the end of each arm and each leg were seven fingers and four thumbs;
at the end of each finger and each thumb
was a very dirty nail.

Sam sat and stared
at the monster
for a long time.

Meanwhile, in the house next door,
Mrs Pollywobble began to chant the magic words:

Fingernails, soup, and all of that,
Send me a creature who'll sit down and chat.
Black is not black,
White is not white,
The place it comes from
Is far beyond night.

Just as she finished, there was a loud thump on the porch and a large cardboard box landed right in front of Mrs Pollywobble. From inside the box came an angry voice, shouting:
'Hey! Let me out of here! Let me out! Hurry up!'

Mrs Pollywobble let out a screech which went through Sam's bedroom window and told him something was very wrong at Mrs Pollywobble's place.

Sam raced outside, scrambled over the fence,
and rushed to Mrs Pollywobble's side.

'Look at that box, Sam!' cried Mrs Pollywobble.
'There's something horrible inside and it's
going to break out!'

The box bulged and bumped until a hole
burst in one side, and through the hole
wriggled a *long* arm with
seven fingers,
                    four thumbs,
                              and
                                   very
                                      dirty
                                         nails . . .

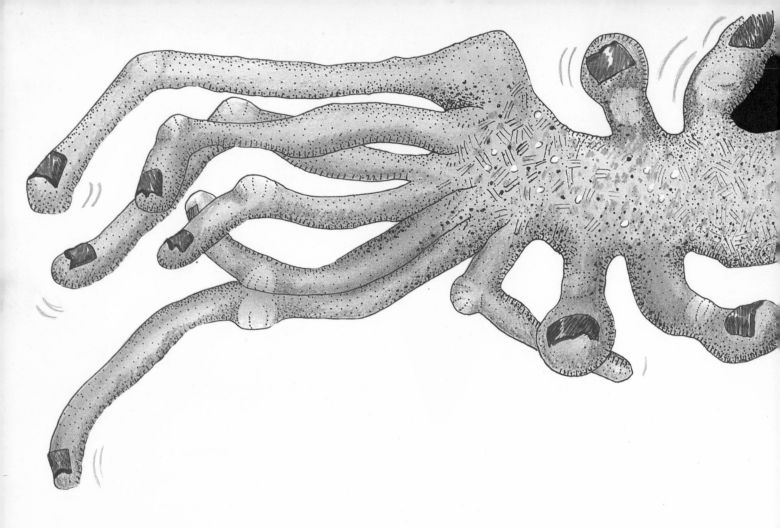

'We mustn't let it escape!' shouted Sam, and they dragged the box into the kitchen. The door slammed behind them.

At that moment, the horror burst out of the box——

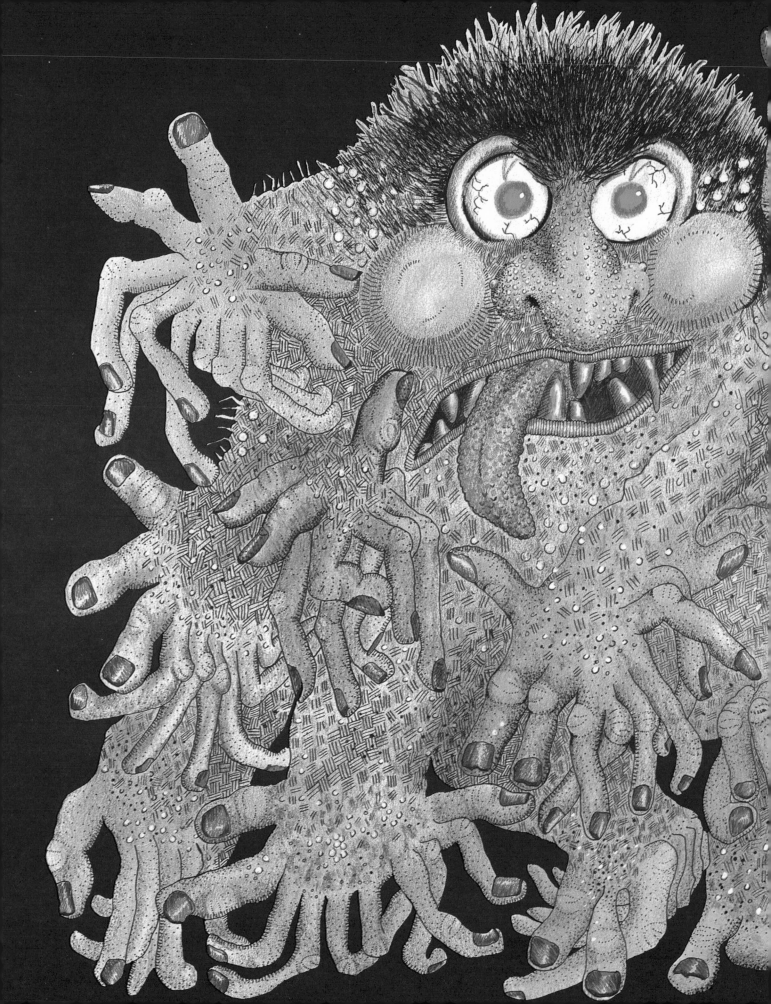

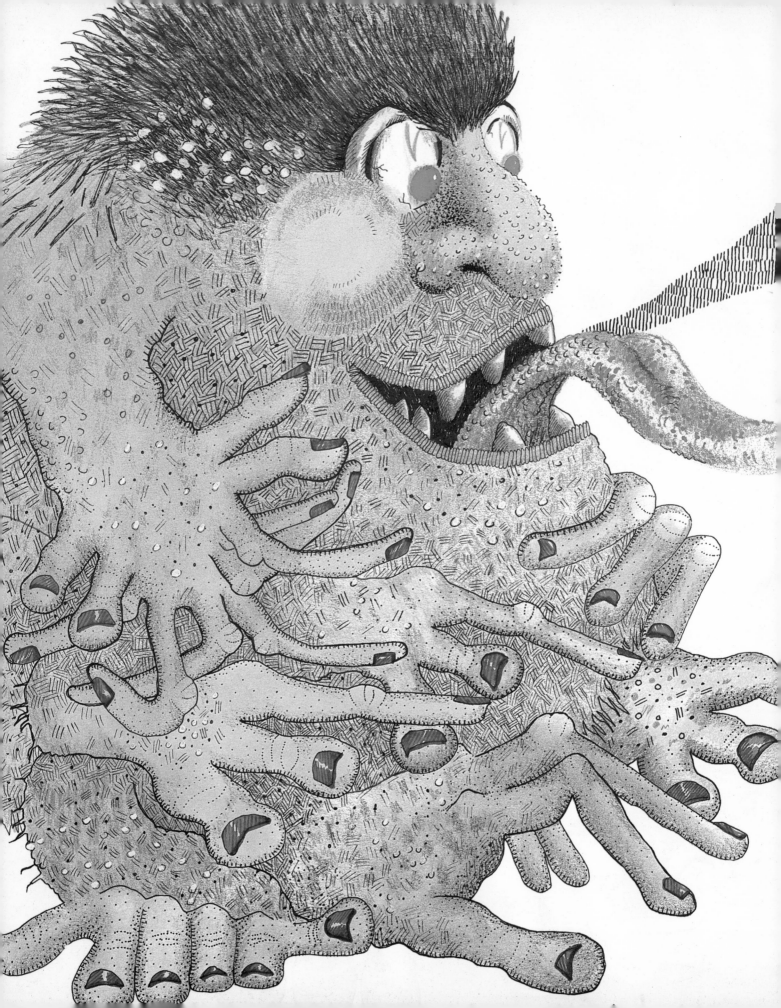

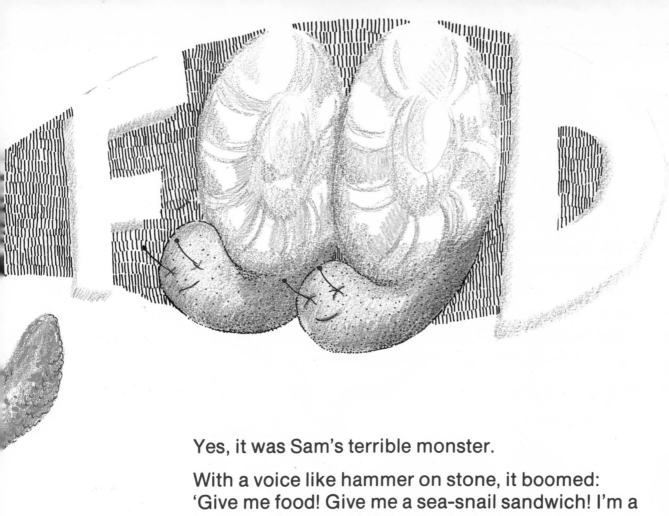

Yes, it was Sam's terrible monster.

With a voice like hammer on stone, it boomed:
'Give me food! Give me a sea-snail sandwich! I'm a
hungry monster, and I'm the laziest monster
you'll ever meet—I hate doing anything for
myself—so hurry up, I want food!'

Mrs Pollywobble and Sam stared in amazement.
'I made a spell to bring me a friendly creature,
not a horrible monster like you,' said
Mrs Pollywobble, getting bolder.

'That's what you thought,' replied the monster
with a nasty grin. 'But I'm smarter than you, and
when I heard you making that spell I dropped in
here to have a holiday. So jump to it!'

Sam could see it was no use arguing, so he raced off down the road to the beach. He dug in the sand and turned over the rocks, but he couldn't find any sea-snails. So back he went to Mrs Pollywobble's garden where he found some garden snails. Then he took some stale bread (which Mrs Pollywobble kept to feed the swans on sunny days) and he made an *enormous* sandwich.

The monster snatched it from him and swallowed it in one gulp.

'Wow!
Your name should be Greedy,'
muttered Sam.

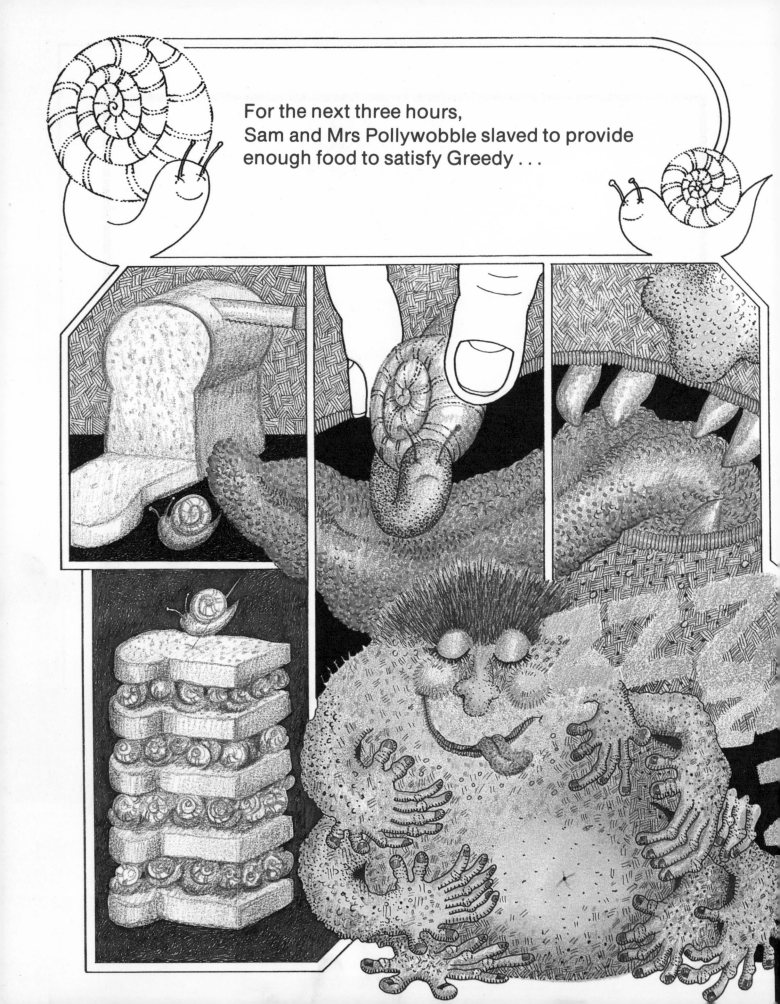

For the next three hours,
Sam and Mrs Pollywobble slaved to provide
enough food to satisfy Greedy . . .

. . . but at long last he fell asleep,
holding his bulging stomach.

Mrs Pollywobble fell into bed,
too weary even to say good-night to Gingerbread.
Sam crept home through his front gate,
too tired even to climb the fence.

First thing next morning,
Sam hurried back to Mrs Pollywobble's place.
He found her arguing with the monster:
'Give me dog's leg on toast!' shouted Greedy.
'No! No!' cried Mrs Pollywobble.
'Never!' cried Sam.
'Fooooooood!' screamed the monster.
'Noooooooo!' yelled Sam.

'Oh dear,' sighed Mrs Pollywobble. 'This is what comes of playing with spells.'

She looked so upset that Sam led her into the front room and sat her in her favourite chair. Gingerbread slunk out from under the chair and leapt into her lap, which made her feel a bit better.

From the kitchen came a voice louder than a jungleful of lions:

'Foooooooood!'

Many streets away, in the town, people heard the monster's roars,
as they did their weekend shopping, bought their lottery tickets
and got ready to go to the football.
'Listen to that terrible noise!' they said. 'Someone should find out what it is.'
'Yes, you go first.'   'No, *you* go first.'
And so they argued, while Mrs Pollywobble's stone house shook
as the monster tramped up and down, shouting for food.

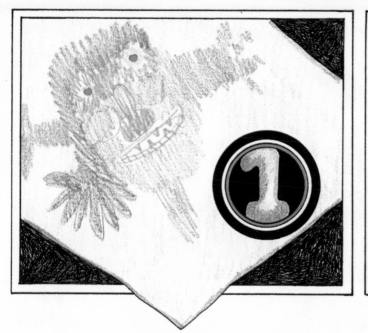

Suddenly, Sam realized exactly what he should do. He raced back to his bedroom, snatched up his drawing pad and rubber, and ran back to the kitchen where the monster raged.
Sam wasn't afraid. He sat down at the kitchen table and quickly set to work.

Like magic, the monster's cries melted into silence.

Mrs Pollywobble rushed in and saw what was happening—
Sam was rubbing out his drawing, bit by bit,
and as the drawing disappeared, so did the monster
in the corner of the kitchen.

'Let me have a turn!' said Mrs Pollywobble,
and she rubbed and rubbed until it was gone—
every ugly line that Sam had drawn, and every
arm, leg, finger, thumb and dirty nail of the greedy monster.

Finally, all that was left was a battered cardboard box.

The kitchen began to feel like home again. Mrs Pollywobble and Sam spent the rest of the day recovering and tidying up the house. That night, when Sam took the box outside with the rubbish, an awful thought struck him.

'What about the **IDEA**, Mrs Pollywobble? We've rubbed out the monster, but the **IDEA** is still loose. Greedy could come back whenever someone tries that spell!'

They searched everywhere, but they couldn't find the **IDEA**.

They were almost ready to give up, when Gingerbread began to wail on the back porch. He had found the IDEA, and there he was, up among the ivy leaves, holding it under his strong paws. (Perhaps he was a witch's cat, after all.)

'We must put it somewhere it can never escape,' said Sam.

So Mrs Pollywobble fetched the big, framed picture of sailing ships which was hanging on her wall. She took out the picture, slipped the IDEA behind the glass, and quickly fastened the frame. It would never escape from here. They were safe.

Sam and Mrs Pollywobble had tea and chocolate biscuits, to celebrate.

Now on some nights, when Mrs Pollywobble looks at her strange cat Gingerbread, or picks up the old book of spells, she sees the IDEA in the picture frame and thinks: 'No more would-be-witching for me. I've got Gingerbread to keep me company, and Sam to talk to me.'

All the same, there *is* one spell she reads rather often. It's called:

'How to make a TRAVEL MACHINE (magic kind)'.

And next door, in his bedroom, Sam draws cars and trains and spaceships.